People in the Community

Dentists

Diyan Leake

Heinemann Library
Chicago, Illinois

Customer Service 888-454-2279
Visit our website at www.heinemannraintree.com

Designed by Joanna Hinton-Malivoire and Steve Mead
Printed in China by South China Printing Company Limited

12 11 10 09 08
10 9 8 7 6 5 4 3 2 1

Library of Congress Cataloguing-in-Publication Data
Leake, Diyan.
  Dentists / Diyan Leake.
     p. cm. -- (People in the community)
  Includes bibliographical references and index.
  ISBN-13: 978-1-4329-1187-4 (hc)
  ISBN-13: 978-1-4329-1194-2 (pb)
  1. Dentists--Vocational guidance--Juvenile literature. 2. Dentistry--Vocational guidance--Juvenile literature. I. Title.
  RK63.L43 2008
  617.6'0232--dc22
                         2007045070

Acknowledgments
The publishers would like to thank the following for permission to reproduce photographs:
©Age Fotostock pp. **4** (Werner Otto), **9** (Sylvain Grandadam) **22 (top)** (Werner Otto); ©Alamy (Peter Griffin) p. **5**; ©Corbis pp. **7** (FotostudioFM/Zefa), **11** (Peter Beck), **16** (Lucidio Studio, Inc.), **17** (Tom Stewart), **20** (Simon Marcus), **22** (Peter Beck); ©Getty Images pp. **8** (Jon Riley), **10** (PNC), **12** (Paul Burns), **13** (Paul Burns), **18** (Wayne Eastep), **19** (Karin Dreyer), **21** (Chabruken); ©Heinemann-Raintree (Tracy Cummins) pp. **14**, **22 (middle)**; ©Jupiter Images (Anderson Ross) p. **6**; ©Robert & Linda Mitchell p. **15**.

Front cover photograph of a dentist reproduced with permission of ©Getty Images. Back cover photograph reproduced with permission of ©Getty Images (Karin Dreyer).

Every effort has been made to contact copyright holders of any material reproduced in this book. Any omissions will be rectified in subsequent printings if notice is given to the publisher.

Contents

Communities

People live in communities.

People work in communities.

Dentists in the Community

Dentists work in communities.

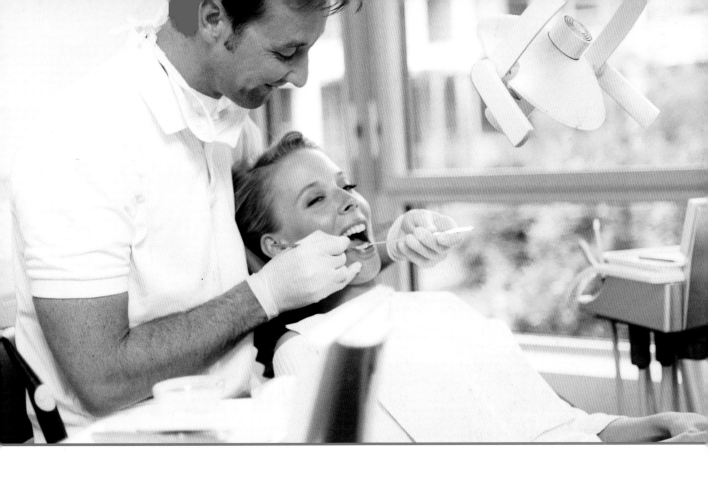

Dentists care for people's teeth.

What Dentists Do

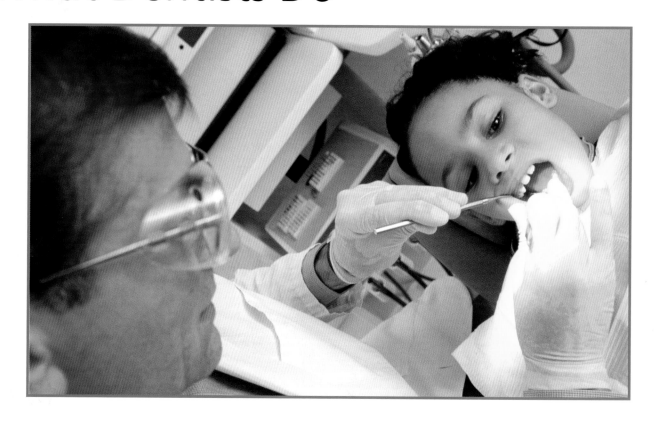

Dentists check people's teeth.

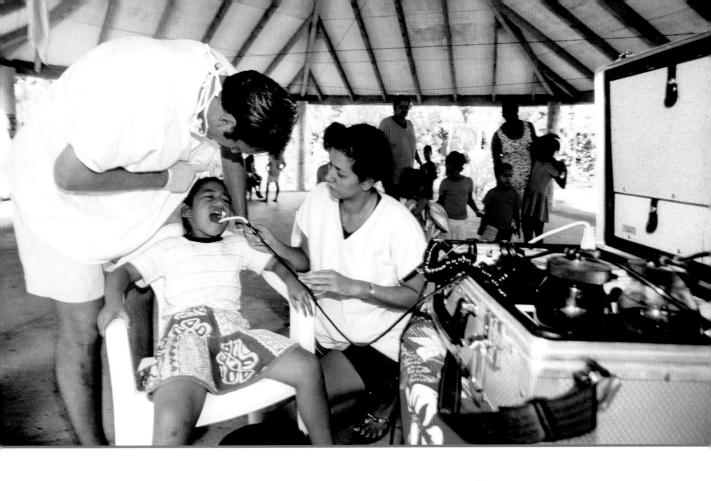

Dentists clean people's teeth.

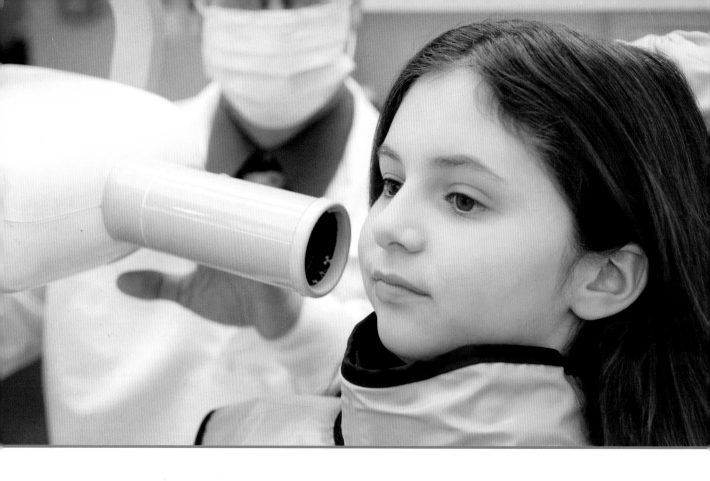

Dentists take X-rays of teeth.

X-rays are pictures of teeth.

What Dentists Use

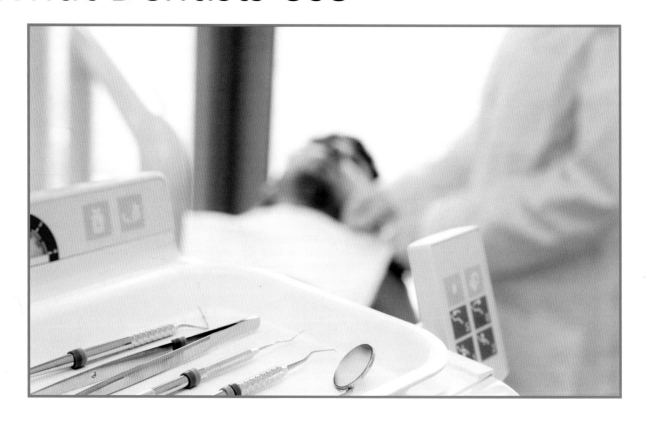

Dentists use tools.

mirror

Dentists use mirrors.

Where Dentists Work

Dentists work in offices.

Dentists work at clinics.

People Who Work with Dentists

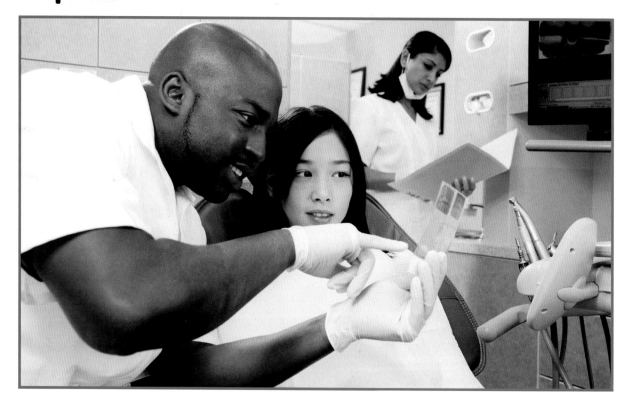

Dentists work with other people.

This person greets people.

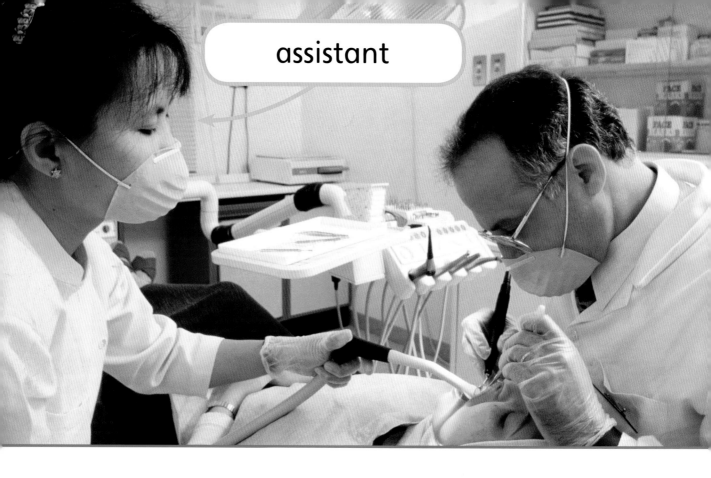

assistant

This person helps the dentist.

hygienist

This person helps clean teeth.

How Dentists Help Us

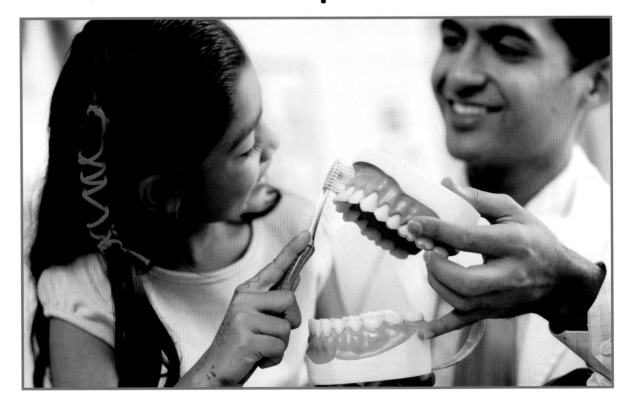

Dentists help keep our teeth healthy.

Dentists help the community.

Picture Glossary

 **community** group of people living and working in the same area

 **office** place where a dentist works

 **X-ray** photo of the inside of a person's body

Index

Note to Parents and Teachers

This series introduces readers to the lives of different community workers, and explains some of the different jobs they perform around the world. Some of the locations featured include Hanover, Germany (page 4); Ua Pou, French Polynesia (page 9); Chicago, IL (page 14), and Siem Reap, Cambodia (page 15).

Discuss with children their experiences with dentists in the community. Do they know any dentists? Have they ever visited a dentist's office? What was it like? Discuss with children why communities need dentists.

Ask children to look through the book and name some of the tools dentists use to help them with their job. Give children poster boards and ask them to draw dentists. Tell them to show the clothes and tools they use to do their job.

The text has been chosen with the advice of a literacy expert to enable beginning readers success while reading independently or with moderate support. You can support children's nonfiction literacy skills by helping them use the table of contents, picture glossary, and index.